CONTENTS

PREFACE

York Notes are designed to give you a broader perspective on works of literature studied at GCSE and equivalent levels. We have carried out extensive research into the needs of the modern literature student prior to publishing this new edition. Our research showed that no existing series fully met students' requirements. Rather than present a single authoritative approach, we have provided alternative viewpoints, empowering students to reach their own interpretations of the text. York Notes provide a close examination of the work and include biographical and historical background, summaries, glossaries, analyses of characters, themes, structure and language, cultural connections and literary terms.

If you look at the Contents page you will see the structure for the series. However, there's no need to read from the beginning to the end as you would with a novel, play, poem or short story. Use the Notes in the way that suits you. Our aim is to help you with your understanding of the work, not to dictate how you should learn.

York Notes are written by English teachers and examiners, with an expert knowledge of the subject. They show you how to succeed in coursework and examination assignments, guiding you through the text and offering practical advice. Questions and comments will extend, test and reinforce your knowledge. Attractive colour design and illustrations improve clarity and understanding, making these Notes easy to use and handy for quick reference.

York Notes are ideal for:
- Essay writing
- Exam preparation
- Class discussion

The author of these Notes is Imelda Pilgrim, a full-time teacher of English in a comprehensive school in the North East of England. She is an English graduate and a Principal Examiner for English.

The text used in these Notes is the Puffin Modern Classics 1995 edition of *Roll of Thunder, Hear My Cry.*

Health Warning: **This study guide will enhance your understanding, but should not replace the reading of the original text and/or study in class.**

PART ONE

INTRODUCTION

HOW TO STUDY A NOVEL

You have bought this book because you wanted to study a novel on your own. This may supplement classwork.

- You will need to read the novel several times. Start by reading it quickly for pleasure, then read it slowly and carefully. Further readings will generate new ideas and help you to memorise the details of the story.
- Make careful notes on themes, plot and characters of the novel. The plot will change some of the characters. Who changes?
- The novel may not present events chronologically. Does the novel you are reading begin at the beginning of the story or does it contain flashbacks and a muddled time sequence? Can you think why?
- How is the story told? Is it narrated by one of the characters or by an all-seeing ('omniscient') narrator?
- Does the same person tell the story all the way through? Or do we see the events through the minds and feelings of a number of different people?
- Which characters does the narrator like? Which characters do you like or dislike? Do your sympathies change during the course of the book? Why? When?
- Any piece of writing (including your notes and essays) is the result of thousands of choices. No book had to be written in just one way: the author could have chosen other words, other phrases, other characters, other events. How could the author of your novel have written the story differently? If events were recounted by a minor character how would this change the novel?

Studying on your own requires self-discipline and a carefully thought-out work plan in order to be effective. Good luck.

Early life   Mildred Taylor, a black American writer, was born in
Jackson, Mississippi in the 1940s. Her father's family
had lived there since the days of slavery. *Roll of
Thunder, Hear My Cry* is dedicated to the memory of
her father who played a very positive role in her life and
'lived many adventures of the boy Stacey and who was
in essence the man David'. Her childhood was spent in
the northern state of Ohio, though she returned to
Mississippi many times. It was through these visits that
she became aware of the inequities of society and the
effects of segregation and racist laws.

Following her graduation from university in 1965, she
spent two years with the Peace Corps – a volunteer aid
organisation – in Ethiopia. On returning to the United
States she entered the School of Journalism at the
University of Colorado, where she helped to structure
a Black Studies programme. Upon completion of
her Master's degree, she worked as a study skills
co-ordinator in the Black Education Programme.

Storytelling   Storytelling was an important part of her family life and
it was from her father's stories that she learnt her
family's history and developed a strong respect both for
the past and for her own heritage. She attributes her
skills as a storyteller to this, saying that it was listening
to her father and uncle tell stories one breakfast that
gave her the idea for *Roll of Thunder, Hear My Cry*.
This storytelling tradition is reflected in the book when
Big Ma tells Cassie the history of the Logan land and
when all the family is sitting round the fire telling
stories on Christmas Eve. Whilst the book is not
strictly autobiographical, Taylor clearly draws on
personal experience in the creation of her characters
(see Literary Terms) and in the depiction of particular
situations.

In *Roll of Thunder, Hear My Cry* Mildred Taylor

portrays the struggles of the Logan family to survive the racism and difficulties around them in Mississippi in the 1930s. She continues to follow the family's fortunes in its sequel *Let the Circle be Unbroken* (1981) and her later novel *The Road to Memphis* (1991).

CONTEXT & SETTING

The novel is set in 1933 in the southern state of Mississippi. To understand the situation of the Logan family and the attitudes and prejudices explored within the story, you need to have some understanding of the historical background.

Slavery in the southern states

The United States of America is formed from a number of states, each of which has its own laws about internal matters. Federal laws, however, are fixed by the President and Congress and apply to all states. In the period prior to the Civil War enormous differences had developed between the northern and southern states. The southern states relied heavily on agriculture, with crops such as cotton, tobacco and rice grown on large farms known as plantations. The land was worked predominantly by black slaves, who had originally been imported from Africa in the seventeenth century. The North was more industrialised and its economy more city-based, with New York forming a major banking centre.

Divisions between the northern and southern states grew, with people in the North increasingly believing that slavery was morally wrong. There was economic conflict as well. Northern manufacturers wanted custom duties put on foreign goods, whilst southern planters wanted free importation of goods. The South feared that it would be defeated in Congress and in 1860, during the Presidency of Abraham Lincoln, the Confederate States of America was formed. This

1 Slavery

- Slaves taken from Africa
- Worked on plantations
- Slave trade abolished in 1807
- Southern states continued to trade illegally
- Many slaves lived in terrible conditions

2 The Civil War: 1861–5

- Fought between northern and southern states
- Southern states defeated
- Slavery finally ended in the South

3 Reconstruction

- Attempts to create a more equal society
- Largely unsuccessful
- 1866: formation of the Ku Klux Klan
- Many atrocities committed against Blacks

4 The Depression: 1930s

- Price of cotton fell dramatically
- Sharecroppers suffered badly
- Unemployment rose rapidly

consisted of several slave keeping states, including Mississippi.

Civil War
1861–1865

In 1861 the Civil War began. Whilst the main aim of the North was to restore the Union, a secondary aim was to free all slaves. The war was long and bitter, dividing families as well as the nation. It continued until 1865, when the southern Confederacy surrendered to the northern general, Ulysses Grant.

Reconstruction

There followed a period of racial adjustment, known as Reconstruction (1865–1877), which was imposed by the North on the South. During this time slavery was ended and four million blacks were granted freedom. This was resented by many of the southern whites, who still believed that black people were fundamentally inferior, as Mama explains to Cassie in Chapter 6

Ku Klux Klan

(pp. 105–8). One product of this resentment was the formation of the Ku Klux Klan in 1866. This was a secret society whose primary aim was to re-establish white supremacy.

Reconstruction was followed by a period of fear and intimidation for black people in the South. Many of the laws that had made them equal were rejected and reversed, and between 1882 and 1903 over 2,000 black people were lynched. Terrible atrocities were committed. Black people were burnt alive, castrated, blinded with hot pokers and decapitated. Pregnant women and children suffered the same fate. This horror is reflected in Mr Morrison's account of the slaughter of his family by the night men in Chapter 7 (pp. 121–4). There were groups of organised 'night men' right up until the 1950s.

The Depression

In the 1930s America was hit by a serious economic depression, started by the Wall Street Crash in 1929. The South was hit very badly by this, with the price of cotton falling dramatically. Cassie refers to this in

Chapter 1 (pp. 11–12) when explaining why Papa went to work on the railroad. One consequence of the Depression was that unemployment rose, creating serious hardship for the majority of people, both black and white alike. In the story we see the uncertainty of employment for Papa on the railroad. When he brings Mr Morrison home he only stays a day for fear of losing his job. Mr Morrison, having been fired from the railroad, has litttle hope of finding alternative employment.

PART TWO

SUMMARIES

GENERAL SUMMARY

The story combines the adult world and the world of the child from the viewpoint of a black girl, Cassie Logan, the narrator of the story, who is growing up in the southern state of Mississippi in the difficult years following the stock market crash of 1929. These are hard times in a state where the black population is already subject to extreme racist attitudes. Cassie, however, has a secure and stable family background and she and her older brother, Stacey, and younger brothers, Christopher John and Little Man, are raised with a clear knowledge of their own self worth and a pride in their family traditions. These are provided for them by Big Ma, their grandmother, and by their Mama, Mary, and Papa, David. Together these three adults create a home for the children in which they are surrounded by love, firm discipline and a strong sense of right and wrong. In the course of the story you are shown how the children are taught to discriminate right from wrong and to have respect both for others and themselves.

The Logan family

The land

The family are unusual in that they own their own land, 400 acres bought by Big Ma and her late husband, Paul Edward. This sets the family apart, giving them economic independence, in contrast to most of their neighbours who are sharecroppers working for little or no profit on the plantations of the wealthy white landowners. The Logans have the freedom to choose to shop in Vicksburg, whereas Mr Avery and Mr Lanier are forced to shop at the local Wallace store when Mr Granger threatens to throw them off his land. The land is central to the story as it represents freedom and choice. Papa and his brother, Uncle Hammer, who works in the more prosperous North where black people have more opportunity, will do anything to ensure it remains in the family.

Racism and
segregation

Through Cassie's eyes, you see the effects of racism at this time. The children are segregated, with white children attending the well-equipped Jefferson Davis County School and black children being taught in the 'weather-beaten wooden houses' (p. 18) of the Great Faith Elementary School. Most of the money supporting this school comes from the black churches, whereas the County funds the school for the white children. White children are provided with a bus to take them to school but the black children have to walk and are frequently showered with dust or mud by the bus driver or humiliated by the racist taunts of the passengers. The black children are not provided with books and are expected to be grateful when they do receive the cast-offs of the white school clearly labelled 'Very Poor – nigra' (p. 26). Cassie is regarded as inferior by Lillian Jean Simms and is expected to not only apologise for bumping into her at Strawberry, but also to call her 'Miz' and to get off the pavement and walk on the road. At the Barnett Mercantile in Strawberry Mr Barnett serves white adults and children first and when Cassie questions this he abusively tells her to get 'her little black self over there and wait some more' (p. 94).

Revenge

The Logan children, following the example of their parents, do not simply accept things the way they are. Stacey leads the others in getting their revenge on the bus and its occupants by digging a deep gully in which the bus becomes stranded, forcing its occupants to wade through mud and water. Little Man refuses to accept his book at school and Cassie stands by him, even though both children are beaten for their disobedience

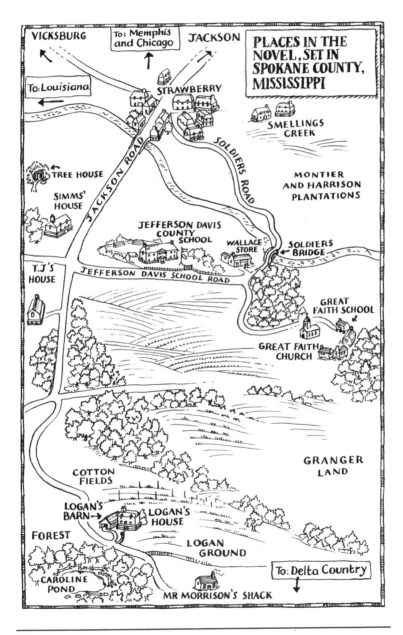

by their teacher, Miss Crocker. Cassie, having taken advice from Papa, pretends to befriend Lillian Jean and, when she has gained her trust, beats her up and forces her to apologise.

The Adult world

There are many parallels between the world of the child and the adult world. Mama is better educated than most of her peers and is a teacher at the school the children attend. When the situation regarding the books is brought to her attention she not only covers over the labels on Cassie's and Little Man's books but on those of her own class at school. She teaches her own version of the truth about American history, not what appears in the approved County textbooks, even though it eventually leads to her dismissal, and it is she who encourages a boycott of the Wallace store. Papa is prepared to stand against Mr Granger and to risk his life to prevent a lynching taking place. Uncle Hammer is the most fiery tempered of the family and has to be stopped by Papa's friend Mr Morrison from visiting Mr Simms after the incident between Cassie and Lillian Jean in Strawberry. He refuses to accept unfair treatment at the hands of whites and enjoys showing off his new car, though Mama is afraid he has gone too far when he drives the Packard over Soldiers Bridge, making the Wallaces wait for him to pass.

Racial violence

The adult world, both past and present, is filled with violence and the children become increasingly aware of this as the story progresses. Mr Morrison tells in hushed tones how his family were attacked and murdered by Rebel soldiers. The Berrys are set alight for allegedly flirting with a white woman and Sam Tatum is tarred and feathered for having implied that Mr Barnett was lying. It is so that her children can appreciate the true horror of this violence that Mama takes the children to see the badly burned Mr Berry. Papa suffers a bullet wound and a broken leg at the hands of the Wallaces, though their injuries, inflicted by Mr Morrison in self-defence, are far more serious. The threat of the night men is ever present and the black community live in fear of being attacked in the night.

At the end of the story the worlds of the child and the adult meet and violence is still present. T.J. Avery, Stacey's wayward friend, is unjustly accused of robbing and injuring the Barnetts. Those responsible, R.W. and Melvin Simms, stand amongst his accusers. The Logan children watch in horror as he and his family are dragged from their home and beaten. The white men intend to lynch T.J., despite the intervention of Mr Jamison. Papa succeeds in stopping the lynching, but only through the desperate measure of setting fire to the cotton, forcing all the people, both black and white, to fight the flames which threaten to destroy the crop on which their livelihoods depend. They are helped ultimately by rain, and indeed the weather is a constant background feature of the story. As the fire is dampened, the children learn that Mr Barnett has died

T.J. and the land

and that T.J. faces possible death. Cassie is deeply distressed by this and cries for both T.J. and the land.

DETAILED SUMMARIES

CHAPTER 1

It is an early October morning and the first day of school for the Logan children. Little Man, the youngest of the four, is only just beginning school and is excited. Cassie, the narrator of the story, finds nothing special in the day and feels imprisoned by her Sunday-best dress and shoes. Stacey, the oldest boy, is pensive and snappy, whilst Christopher-John cannot stop himself

The land

whistling cheerfully. In the distance the children see the boundary of the Logan land and you learn the importance of the land to the Logan family and of the sacrifices that are made so that the land may be maintained.

THE BUS AND THE NIGHT MEN

On their way to school, the children are joined by
T.J. Avery and his younger brother Claude, who are
clearly poorer than the Logan children and whose
family are sharecroppers on the Granger land. The
subjects of violence and racism are raised by T.J. when
he tells the children how, the previous night, a group of
The Berrys are white men set fire to the Berrys. The children seem less
attacked. horrified by this than you may be and the subject is
soon changed. T.J. boasts of how he goes to the
Wallace store and of how he managed to escape a
beating from his mother by blaming his younger
brother Claude.

All the children, except Little Man, get off the road
quickly as the white children's school bus approaches.
Little Man is covered with red dust and is deeply upset.
Stacey is furious on his behalf. Soon after, the children
are joined by a young white boy called Jeremy, who
chooses to walk part of the way to school with the black
children rather than catch the bus. Jeremy attends the
Jefferson Davis County School while the Logan
children go to the Great Faith Elementary and
Secondary School. The schools have different terms
because the black children have to help throughout the
cotton picking season, and the contrasts in the
buildings and grounds forcefully reflect the differing
resources on which each relies.

Little Man, who is in the first grade, and Cassie, who is
in the fourth grade, are in the same classroom. Miss
'New' books Daisy Crocker welcomes the children in a patronising
fashion and announces that this year they will each have
a book. The children's initial excitement turns to
disappointment when they see that the books are dirty
and badly worn and portray images of white children.
Little Man, infuriated by the realisation that his book is
considered to be unfit for white children, flings it to the
floor and stamps on it. Cassie tries, unsuccessfully, to

Y

explain his reaction to Miss Crocker and, supporting her brother, she too refuses to keep her book. Both children are beaten by Miss Crocker.

Later Cassie overhears Miss Crocker telling Mama about their behaviour. Mama does not openly criticise Miss Crocker but clearly understands her children's objections. She sticks new labels on their books and also on the books of the seventh grade pupils.

COMMENT   We are introduced to each of the Logan children and learn something of their individual characters (see Literary Terms). Cassie, in particular, is portrayed as having a strong and independent spirit. Whilst the children do argue, they stand up for each other in times of trouble.

The Logan family are different from many of their neighbours in that they own the land on which they work. Papa makes clear to Cassie that the land is central to their existence. It represents the family's independence and is an important feature throughout the story.

Is Cassie unfairly   Cassie is the narrator of the story and it is through her
prejudiced against   eyes that we first see T.J. Neither she nor Little Man
Stacey's friend   likes him, though he is a close friend of Stacey. He has
T.J.?   failed his last year at school and is already planning to cheat his way through this year. He sensationalises the news of the Berrys and lies to his mother about going to the Wallace store.

The contrast between the educational facilities for the white and the black children is heavily emphasised. The white children have good buildings, a sports field, a large front lawn and a school bus, whilst the black children are educated in run-down wooden houses and have to walk to school. The issue of the books is important because it demonstrates the contempt with which the black pupils are treated. Even when conditions are this bad there are some children, such as Moe, who will walk for seven hours a day in their determination to be educated.

The courage to try to change things

The importance of attitude is made clear from the very start of this story. There are those who accept things as they are and do nothing, such as Miss Crocker. In contrast, there is Mama who seeks to change what little she can by putting labels on the books to cover the offensive table.

GLOSSARY

sharecropping families families who worked on the plantations of white landowners. They were paid a share of the money that the crop earned, but this was often needed to settle the bills for that year's purchases, leaving the families with no clear profit. This is an important factor later in the story when Papa tries to encourage other families to shop in Vicksburg

Reconstruction (1865–1877) the period of racial adjustment imposed by the North on the South after the Civil War. It was widely resented by the whites and many of the rights achieved for the blacks were lost in subsequent years

Yankee a term used by people in the South to describe someone from the North

mortgage property is put forward as security against a loan. If the debt is not paid then the property is forfeited

In 1930 the price of cotton dropped in 1929 the American stock market crashed. This led to the Great Depression, in which extreme poverty afflicted large parts of the country. As a result, the price of cotton fell

burnin' colloquial name for pouring kerosene over someone and setting them alight. Such attacks by whites against blacks were common

towheaded someone with blond or yellowish hair

Jefferson Davis County School Jefferson Davis was the president of the Confederate states and led them in the Civil War

Confederacy the name given to the group of seven states who left the Union of states in 1860, one of the decisive actions which gave rise to the Civil War

plantations the huge farms on which the cotton is grown. At one time the plantations were run on slave labour

fall (*American usage*) autumn

nigra a derogatory word used to describe black people, derived from the Spanish word 'negro', meaning the colour black

CHAPTER 2   Cassie and the other members of the Logan family are picking cotton on the land. You sense the danger in this from Big Ma's concern for the children. In the distance Cassie sees two men approaching and realises that one of these is her father. Accompanying him is Mr Morrison who is, according to Cassie, the 'most formidable-looking being' she has ever seen (p. 33). Papa is clearly delighted to see his wife and children. The group move towards the house and Mr Morrisonis impressed by the homely scene that meets his eyes. Papa explains that, having received Mama's letter (which presumably contained news of the Berry burnings), he has brought Mr Morrison home to stay with the family. Mr Morrison has lost his job because he was involved in a fight with some white men.

Why does no one directly accuse the Wallaces of having attacked the Berrys?

The following day the family go to church where it is announced that Mr John Berry has died. The children learn more details of the incident and discover that, despite Henrietta's approach to the sheriff, nobody will be charged with the attack on the Berrys. Papa says that his family do not shop at the Wallace store. He tells the children that the Wallace store is a bad place and forbids them to go there with the prophetic warning that children who do will end up in 'a whole lot of trouble' (p. 39).

THE BUS AND THE NIGHT MEN

COMMENT   Through the response of the children to their father's arrival, we learn more about the closeness of the Logan family.

Mr Morrison is welcomed into the Logan family, the decision of the father to bring him home being unquestioned.

No justice for black people   You learn something of the powerlessness of the black community in the face of gross injustice. The sheriff ignores Henrietta's evidence altogether, calling her a liar, and no effort is made to bring the white men who perpetrated this crime to justice.

Papa's decision not to shop at the Wallace store is reminiscent of Mama's action with the books. Neither of them is prepared to simply accept what has happened. They set an example for their children by their refusal to sit back and do nothing.

GLOSSARY   **pecan** smooth oval nut of the hickory tree, which is pinkish brown in colour

burlap bag bag made from a coarse fabric

ginned the process of freeing seeds from raw cotton, using a machine known as a gin

chiffonier a wide, low, open-fronted cabinet

bootleg liquor alcohol, made or sold illegally during the period of Prohibition in the USA (1920–33). The term came from smugglers concealing bottles of liquor in their boots

switch flexible rod or twig, used especially for punishment. The Logan parents believe in using corporal punishment to discipline their children. Whilst this would be frowned upon nowadays, it was a widespread practice in the 1930s

CHAPTER 3   It is late October and the rain is falling heavily. The children's journey to school is made more difficult by the driver of the Jefferson Davis school bus, who delights in splashing them. Little Man becomes increasingly angry about this. One morning, when the rain is very heavy, the children are forced into the slime of a gully. Little Man is driven to tears when he hears the white children's taunts of 'Nigger! Nigger! Mud eater!' (p. 44). When Jeremy unwittingly runs to join the group of children he takes the force of Stacey's anger. It is only then that Cassie realises that Jeremy never travels on the bus.

'Nigger! Nigger! Mud eater!'

Stacey is determined to get revenge and arranges to meet the other children at lunch time in the toolshed. Once there, they grab buckets and shovels and return to the point where the bus forced them off the road. They dig frantically, creating a deep ditch and marking the spot with three rocks. By evening the ditch has been transformed into a twelve foot wide lake. The children watch in delight as the bus is marooned, leaving its driver furious and its occupants with no choice but to clamber through the mud.

Ambushing the bus

That night the children can hardly keep from laughing and only become quiet when Mama threatens to send Cassie to the cold kitchen. Their merriment is soon broken, however, with the visit of Mr Avery and his warning that 'They's ridin' t'night' (p. 54). By 'they' he means the night men and the implication of what he

THE BUS AND THE NIGHT MEN

Is it convincing that Cassie should be alone when she witnesses the arrival of the night men?

says is that there could be trouble. The children are sent to bed but do not sleep, believing that the night men are searching for them. Cassie witnesses the arrival of the cars and watches in terror as a man gets out of a car and walks up the drive. Then he shakes his head and the cars turn round and speed away. Greatly shaken, she turns, only to see the shadowy figure of Mr Morrison moving silently from the house to the road with a shotgun in his hand. Quickly she returns to her bed and falls into a restless sleep.

COMMENT

The white bus driver and Jefferson Davis school children take great delight in taunting the black children, using the word 'nigger' as an insult. Jeremy is shown in clear contrast to them, choosing not to travel on the bus but to accompany the Logan children instead.

There is a lack of money for black education.

We see more evidence of the lack of financial support for the education of the black children. There is no money for a school bus and, as Mama makes clear, black schools are mostly paid for by the black churches.

The strength of the Logan family bond is shown by Stacey's anger on behalf of Little Man. It is because of the hurt done to his little brother that Stacey is so determined to wreak revenge.

Just like their Mama and Papa, the children do something to fight back against injustice. It will not prevent such things happening again but they, at least, are not simply accepting the treatment they have received.

Terror of the night men

You are given an insight into the terror created in the community by the night men. It is not only the children who are frightened. Mr Avery's warning and the subsequent actions of Mama, Big Ma and Mr Morrison demonstrate the very real threat the night men pose to all black people.

Y

coddling treating indulgently or spoiling
'ifn meaning 'if only'
gullies channels cut by flooding rainwater
hickory type of tree whose wood is used on fires
They's ridin' t'night a reference to the night men
kerosene (*American usage*) paraffin; a highly flammable oil
normally used for heating or in lights
night men the white men who drive in groups at night and
cause trouble

TEST YOURSELF (Chapters 1–3)

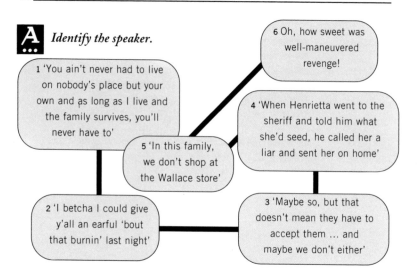

A *Identify the speaker.*

6 Oh, how sweet was well-maneuvered revenge!

1 'You ain't never had to live on nobody's place but your own and as long as I live and the family survives, you'll never have to'

4 'When Henrietta went to the sheriff and told him what she'd seed, he called her a liar and sent her on home'

5 'In this family, we don't shop at the Wallace store'

2 'I betcha I could give y'all an earful 'bout that burnin' last night'

3 'Maybe so, but that doesn't mean they have to accept them ... and maybe we don't either'

Identify the person(s) 'to whom' this comment refers.

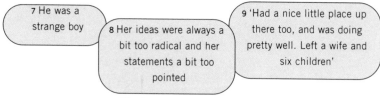

7 He was a strange boy

8 Her ideas were always a bit too radical and her statements a bit too pointed

9 'Had a nice little place up there too, and was doing pretty well. Left a wife and six children'

Check your answers on page 80.

B *Consider these issues.*

a The advantages and disadvantages of telling a story from a child's point of view.

b What we learn about the Logan children and their sense of family.

c How T.J. is presented to us in the early stages of the story.

d The evidence of racial discrimination within the education system.

e The history of the land and its importance to the Logan family.

f How Mama and Papa teach their children to be good people.

g The presence of Jeremy and what he might represent in the author's eyes.

h What we have learned so far about the structure of the society and how that structure is maintained.

CHAPTER 4   The children continue to worry about the night men
until T.J. reveals the reason for the night ride. They
had tarred and feathered Mr Sam Tatum for supposedly
accusing a white man of lying. Mr Morrison has settled
into the empty shack in the south pasture and the
children feel safer for his being there. Stacey, however,
resents his presence, believing he is capable of looking
after the family by himself.

T.J. cheats in the   T.J. attempts to cheat in the History test and Stacey
History test.   gets the blame. Stacey experiences the humiliation of
being 'whipped' by his own mother. After school T.J.
flees to the Wallace store and Stacey follows him. Even
though Pa has forbidden them to go there, the other
children reluctantly follow. T.J. and Stacey fight,
oblivious to the arrival of Mr Morrison, who pulls
Stacey off T.J. and orders all the children back to the
wagon. He leaves it to them to decide whether to tell
Mama what has happened and Stacey, seeing the
fairness of what he has said, agrees to do so.

To what extent   They arrive home to find that Big Ma has been visited
are the fallen trees   by Mr Granger. Big Ma and Cassie walk to the forest
a symbol of the   where Mr Anderson had chopped down many trees
threat posed by   without her consent. She tells Cassie the story of the
white people?   land and how she and Cassie's grandfather struggled to
buy it. It is a story that Cassie already knows well. Big
Ma explains how the land is in their blood and they will
not sell it.

Stacey tells Mama about going to the Wallace Store.
Mama is upset and the following Saturday takes the
children to see Mr Berry, the man set on fire by the
night men. The full horror of that event is brought
home to the children as they gaze on his frighteningly
disfigured face. On the way back Mama tells the
children that the Wallaces were responsible for this.
They stop at the homes of some of the students and

Mama asks the parents to keep their children away from the store. Many would like to avoid it altogether, but cannot afford to shop elsewhere. Mr Turner says he would be willing to shop in Vicksburg if credit could be arranged.

COMMENT   Through Cassie's talk with Big Ma, you discover more about the history of the land and its importance to the family.

Responsibility   Stacey learns a useful lesson about taking responsibility for his actions and his admiration for Mr Morrison increases.

T.J. is shown not only as a cheat, but also as a coward who is prepared to let a friend take the blame for him.

Mama teaches the children a difficult but essential lesson. By taking them to see Mr Berry, she shows them just how bad the Wallaces are.

No economic freedom   You are shown the financial constraints imposed on most of the black community. They do not have the economic freedom to boycott the Wallace store because they are unable to get credit elsewhere.

GLOSSARY   **snippety** sharp or sarcastic

Mercantile a shop or store

W.E.B. Du Bois's *The Negro* written in 1915, this book challenged many of the stereotypes of black people presented in white American literature. It is significant that Mama should be using this book in her teaching

clapboard long, thin timber board used for house construction

checkers American name for the game of draughts

two years 'fore freedom come slaves were freed in 1865 by the passing of an amendment to the Constitution of the United States

Confederate money money which was no longer of any value

'Old South' the rich landowners in the southern states who gained most under the old system

Y

CHAPTER 5

Cassie goes to the market in Strawberry.

For Cassie, the day starts with great excitement as she learns that she is finally going to accompany Big Ma to the market in Strawberry. Even the presence of T.J. does not diminish her hopes for the day ahead. It is a day, however, of disappointments and humiliation, starting with the town itself, which does not live up to her expectations. Then she is confused by Big Ma's choice of pitch at the distant and least accessible end of the market. She does not understand why the white people should have the best positions. After the sale she is refused permission to go and see Mr Jamison, the attorney, whom she likes for the respect he shows her family.

Against Big Ma's orders she accompanies T.J. and Stacey to the store and is appalled to find that the storekeeper, Mr Barnett, serves the white people before the black. When she tackles him about this he becomes angry shouting 'Whose little nigger is this!' (p. 94). Stacey, angry at what has happened, has to drag her out of the store.

How does the author ensure that our sympathies lie with Cassie?

The final straw comes for Cassie when she bumps into Lillian Jean on the side walk and Lillian Jean, having got her apology, orders Cassie to walk on the road. The scene becomes ugly and dangerous as Mr Simms,

LESSONS TO LEARN

Lillian Jean's father, grabs hold of Cassie and insists she does as his daughter has ordered. At this point Big Ma comes along and reluctantly commands Cassie to apologise again and to call Lillian Jean 'Miz'. Cassie has no choice but to comply and returns to the wagon in tears.

COMMENT

Cassie is learning essential but hard lessons about life for a black person. She has a strong sense of her own worth and resents the unfairness of the situations she faces.

T.J. is described by Stacey as someone who knows how to handle things. T.J. says he would sell his life for a gun like the pearl-handled one, almost as though he is foretelling the future.

Lillian Jean demonstrates the blind prejudice of her father while Jeremy stands by, watching helplessly.

Mr Barnett recoils when Cassie touches him as though he is physically repelled by her presence. He speaks to her with total contempt, taking no account of her age.

Humiliation at the hands of white people.

Both Stacey and Big Ma have to humble themselves in front of a white person and Cassie is compelled to do the same. The threatening and dangerous nature of the situation is made clear to you by the fear in Big Ma's eyes.

GLOSSARY

clabber milk curdled milk

flour-sack-cut dresses unfashionable, badly cut dresses with little shape or style

sidewalk (*American usage*) pavement

cuttin' up making trouble or being a nuisance

CHAPTER 6

The children are delighted to find that their Uncle Hammer has arrived for his Christmas visit and that he has a shiny silver Packard which is newer than Mr

Granger's. Despite Big Ma's efforts to prevent her, Cassie tells her uncle all about the humiliations of the day. Uncle Hammer, seeing the hurt in Cassie's eyes, is furious and leaves hastily, ignoring the protests of Big Ma and Mama. As he gets into his car, determined to go and see Mr Simms, Mr Morrison gets in with him.

To what extent is the author speaking through Mama in her explanation of racism?

Cassie is sent to bed and Mama comes into the room to talk to her. She explains Big Ma's action and the underlying reasons for the prejudice of people such as Mr Simms.

The following morning Uncle Hammer is in the kitchen when Cassie gets up and she learns from Stacey that he has spent the night talking to Mr Morrison. Stacey tells her that Uncle Hammer might have been killed if he had gone to see Mr Simms.

Stacey's wool coat

Uncle Hammer takes the family to church in his new car, having first given Stacey a brand new wool coat. T.J. is jealous and taunts Stacey about looking like a preacher. Stacey pretends not to be bothered, but is obviously hurt.

Snubbing the Wallaces at Soldiers Bridge.

After church the family go for a long drive in the new car. As they approach Soldiers Bridge they see an old Model-T truck reach it first. Uncle Hammer speeds up and the occupants of the truck, believing it is Mr Granger approaching, back off. As the Logan family draw near the Wallaces touch their hats in a mark of respect, only to realise their mistake too late. Mama is concerned that one day they will have to pay for the joke Uncle Hammer has just played on the Wallaces.

COMMENT

Cassie has been brought up to believe in justice and cannot understand why she should either accept or keep quiet about what happened in Strawberry. She feels that Big Ma has let her down and is childlike in her triumph when she manages to tell her story.

LESSONS TO LEARN

The differences between Papa and Uncle Hammer.

Uncle Hammer is different to Papa. Hammer has a fiery temper and acts rashly. Mama and Big Ma are right to fear for his safety, understanding what can happen to a black man in Mississippi if he goes after a white man carrying a gun. Similarly, Mama is right to fear the consequences of Uncle Hammer's action at Soldiers Bridge.

Uncle Hammer is so angry about what has happened to Cassie partly because he feels her hurt, but also because both he and his brother, John Henry, had fought as American soldiers in the First World War. His brother had died and he sees his sacrifice as being a wasted one.

Mama guides Cassie and you, the reader, to a better understanding of racial prejudice. She talks about the history of slavery and explains how white landowners justified it by saying that black people were not like white people. Some white people, like the Simms, she argues, still hold on to that belief because it gives them a (false) sense of superiority.

T.J. is jealous of Stacey's coat.

T.J. tells Stacey he looks like a preacher because he is jealous of his new coat. He acts with bitterness and spite, encouraging the other children to join him in his laughter, and Stacey is clearly upset by this unprovoked attack from his friend.

GLOSSARY

muffle to prevent the expression of something

German war the First World War (1914–1918)

red-neck disparaging term for a poor, uneducated white farm worker

but his owners had not tried to break him in the way a farmer might break a horse to tame its spirit

chignon arrangement of long hair in a roll or knot at the back of the head

Rebel soldiers the Confederate soldiers who fought for the South

Yankee Army the northern forces

TEST YOURSELF (Chapters 4–6)

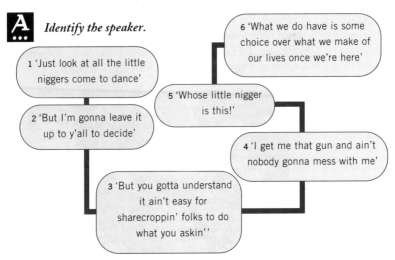

A *Identify the speaker.*

1 'Just look at all the little niggers come to dance'

2 'But I'm gonna leave it up to y'all to decide'

3 'But you gotta understand it ain't easy for sharecroppin' folks to do what you askin''

5 'Whose little nigger is this!'

6 'What we do have is some choice over what we make of our lives once we're here'

4 'I get me that gun and ain't nobody gonna mess with me'

Identify the person(s) 'to whom' this comment refers.

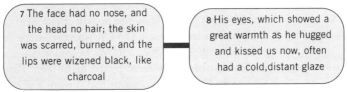

7 The face had no nose, and the head no hair; the skin was scarred, burned, and the lips were wizened black, like charcoal

8 His eyes, which showed a great warmth as he hugged and kissed us now, often had a cold, distant glaze

Check your answers on page 80.

B *Consider these issues.*

a What more you learn about the night men from the latest atrocity.

b What Stacey learns from Mr Morrison and his handling of the incident at the Wallace store.

c Big Ma's personal account of the history of the land and its central place in the history of the family.

d The likely effects of the visit to Mr Berry on the children.

e The difficulties of sharecropping, and why the Logans are considered more fortunate than Mr Turner.

f How the events at Strawberry add to our understanding of the position of black people in this society.

g Mama's attempt to explain, but not justify, the unfairness that Cassie has experienced.

h What we learn about Uncle Hammer.

BLACK AND WHITE

CHAPTER 7 Stacey has given his new coat to T.J. He learns a valuable lesson when Uncle Hammer says that, as Stacey did not have the sense to hang on to something that was rightfully his, T.J. can keep the coat.

Why does the author have Mr Morrison telling his family history at this particular time?

As Christmas approaches Cassie looks forward to the arrival of her father, knowing he will advise her on how to deal with Lillian Jean. On Christmas Eve the adults tell stories about the past and Mr Morrison reveals how his family were slaughtered by the night men. Later that night Cassie is awoken by bad dreams and overhears the adults talking about the land. Her father reassures her that they are never going to lose the land.

Christmas morning

On Christmas morning the children receive a new book each and clothes. Jeremy arrives, bringing nuts for Mama and a handmade flute for Stacey. It is an awkward visit for all concerned and after he leaves Papa explains to Stacey that it is difficult for whites and blacks to be real friends. Stacey puts the flute carefully away, refusing to be riled by T.J.'s derogatory comments.

Before setting off for Vicksburg the following day, Papa beats the children for having disobeyed him and gone to the Wallace store. That afternoon Mr Jamison arrives with the documents necessary for Big Ma to sign over the land to her sons. He offers to back the credit needed to shop in Vicksburg, but warns the Logans that many people, particularly Harlan Granger, will resent what they are doing and that ultimately they can't win. Papa accepts this, but adds that they have to try for the sake of the children.

Shopping in Vicksburg

In the following days Papa and Uncle Hammer take orders for shopping in Vicksburg and return with the goods. Mr Granger comes to the house accusing them of stirring things up and making veiled threats about the mortgage being called in. It is clear that he is not happy with the situation and intends to change it.

COMMENT

Uncle Hammer ignores Big Ma's request that he should let Stacey fetch his coat because he wants to teach Stacey something about the world in which he must grow up – a world where a man must hold fast to his beliefs and not be swayed by the jibes and opinions of others. It is a difficult lesson for Stacey to learn, but he acts on it at later stages in the novel.

The importance of storytelling

Storytelling is an important part of the Logan family tradition and also of the author's. The Christmas Eve scene is a happy and comfortable one. Through storytelling the older members of the family share their memories with the younger generation and teach them important truths about slavery and the injustices carried out by whites against blacks.

Papa's advice to Stacey not to pursue the friendship with Jeremy is based on his belief that this relationship will change as the two boys grow older and will be impossible to sustain in the face of social pressure against it.

Mr Jamison wants to help the Logans because he does not approve of the injustice of the current situation. He acknowledges that amongst whites he is in a minority, but would gain personal satisfaction from doing something that might challenge the way things are.

Mr Granger's objections to the Logans' actions stem from resentment that they own land which once belonged to his family and from a fundamental belief in the inferiority of blacks. He sees their action as a direct accusation against the Wallaces. This carries both the implication that the Wallaces ought to be punished for killing a black man and the assertion of equality.

GLOSSARY   **coon** a raccoon, an animal something like a badger

shantytown area of a town or city where the poor people live in makeshift cabins and shacks

sabers American spelling of 'sabre' – a cavalry sword with a curved blade

kilt killed

collateral security pledged for the repayment of a loan. Because they own the land, the Logans would be able to use it to back the debts of the sharecroppers. However, if the debts were not repaid, the Logans would lose the land

The Count of Monte Cristo ... The Three Musketeers both books were written by Alexandre Dumas (1802–1870), a French writer who had one white and one black parent and whose grandmother was a slave

Aesop's Fables short stories with a clear moral message written by Aesop, a Phrygian born in c.570BC. He was originally a slave but was given his freedom by his master

vest waistcoat

citified with the appearance and habits of someone from the city

Yankee carpetbaggers insulting name for those from the North who came to the South looking to make a profit, the implication being that everything they owned could be carried in a carpet bag

         y

CHAPTER 8

Revenge on Lillian Jean

Having talked to her father, Cassie plans her revenge on Lillian Jean. Much to the surprise of her brothers and Jeremy she starts to pander to Lillian Jean, offering to carry her bag and calling her 'Miz'. Only Stacey seems to realise that she is up to something and forbids the others to say anything to their Mama. Cassie carries on this pretence throughout January. When the exams have finished she shows her true colours, enticing Lillian Jean to a quiet spot in the woods and then proceeding to beat her into submission. Having learnt all Lillian Jean's intimate secrets, she then uses these to blackmail her into saying nothing about what has happened. Cassie is genuinely puzzled by Lillian Jean's failure to see that she has been tricked.

Are the school board members right to insist that Mama should follow the set curriculum?

T.J. is caught cheating in his final exams and is furious with Mrs Logan. He goes off to the Wallace store where, according to Little Willie, he tells people that Mrs Logan wasn't a good teacher and has destroyed school property. As a result of this she receives a visit from Kaleb Wallace and Mr Granger who are both members of the school board. She is fired on the pretext that she is not teaching the children correctly. This is a personal blow for Mama, who loves teaching, and also for the family, who need her wages to make ends meet. Mr Morrison offers to find work elsewhere but Papa assures him that he is needed there.

The children are furious with T.J. and decide they will not associate with him anymore. He is also spurned by the other children at school. When he realises they are not going to change their minds he becomes angry and says that he has better friends anyway and that they are white.

COMMENT

Papa's wisdom shows in the advice he gives to Cassie. Because of it, she finds a way to fight back against injustice without causing difficulties for her father.

BLACK AND WHITE

Lillian Jean genuinely does not understand the apparent change in Cassie. She regards her subservient behaviour as normal and her bewildered reaction takes some of the pleasure away from Cassie's victory. Through this the author suggests that Lillian Jean is also a victim of the prevailing attitudes of the society in which she lives.

Mr Granger makes life difficult.

Mama is officially dismissed for being subversive, for teaching the children a version of history which does not appear in the state curriculum and for covering up the chart on the inside of the books. It is clear, however, that the real reason is because ·Mr Granger wishes to make life difficult for the Logan family.

The closeness and warmth of the Logan family is again demonstrated by Papa's concern for his wife and the support and understanding he shows her when she loses the job that means so much to her.

T.J. is becoming isolated.

The betrayal of Mama by T.J. marks the start of his increasing isolation and the beginning of his disastrous friendship with the Simms brothers. T.J. himself has no real understanding of the enormity of what he has done.

GLOSSARY

Uncle Tomming a reference to a book called *Uncle Tom's Cabin* by Harriet Beecher Stowe (1811–96). When it was written in 1852 it was regarded as a great anti-slavery novel, but by the twentieth century the main character, Uncle Tom, was considered to represent slavish servility

doggone an exclamation of annoyance

flat braids hair tightly plaited against the head

sassed answered cheekily

Board of Education the body in charge of school funding and school curriculum

Delta the southern delta area of Mississippi

Y

CHAPTER 9   It is spring and for the black children the end of the
school year is close to hand, though the white children
continue schooling until mid-May. Jeremy reveals that
his brothers, R.W. and Melvin, are friendly with T.J.
on the surface but laugh at him behind his back. Mr
Jamison comes to tell Papa that Thurston Wallace has
been threatening to stop the shopping in Vicksburg.

Pressure
on the
sharecroppers

Papa decides he must return to the railroad after the
next shopping trip to Vicksburg. Mr Avery and Mr
Lanier tell Papa that they can no longer shop at
Vicksburg because Mr Granger has increased his
demands from 50 to 60 per cent of their cotton.
Amongst the plantation owners only Mr Harrison has
not raised the percentage. Mr Granger has also told the
sharecroppers that if they don't stop shopping at
Vicksburg they must leave his land. The Wallaces have
put additional pressure on them by threatening that if
they don't pay their debts they will call the sheriff in
and have them placed on the chain gang. After the men
have left, Stacey angrily calls them a bunch of 'scared
jackrabbits' (p. 165), but Papa quickly points out that
they have no choice.

In what ways is
Stacey likely to be
affected by the
frightening events
of the evening?

Papa decides to take Stacey to Vicksburg with him,
though Mama is worried for his safety. They discuss
T.J. and agree that he has got out of hand. There are
still seven families who refuse to shop at the Wallace
store. Papa, Stacey and Mr Morrison set out on the
Wednesday morning. They are late returning on the
Thursday and when they do Papa is badly injured with
a broken leg and a bullet wound to his head. Stacey is
tired and clearly shocked. He tells the other children
how, on the way home, both back wheels had come off
the wagon and then they were attacked by three men
who had been following them in a truck. The men shot
Papa as he was trying to mend the wheels and the
wagon rolled onto his leg. Mr Morrison saved them by

overwhelming the three men. Stacey said he thought the men were Wallaces.

COMMENT   The focus is turned on T.J. by Jeremy's revelations about his brothers' treatment of him and by Mama's and Papa's concerns that Stacey should not go the same way. It is clear that T.J. is mixing with bad company and that something will happen in the near future.

Our attention is drawn to the helplessness of the black sharecroppers by the situation of Mr Lanier and Mr Avery. Their economic dependence on the white landowners means they have no real freedom to express their discontent.

A deliberate attack   The attack on Papa, Stacey and Mr Morrison was clearly planned, Stacey having seen two boys messing with the wagon in Vicksburg. It is implied that both Papa and Stacey would have been in even more danger had Mr Morrison not managed to overcome the attackers.

GLOSSARY   **persnickety** (*American usage*) pernickety or fussy

amenities civilities

chain gang group of convicts chained together, usually doing hard labour

sassy saucy

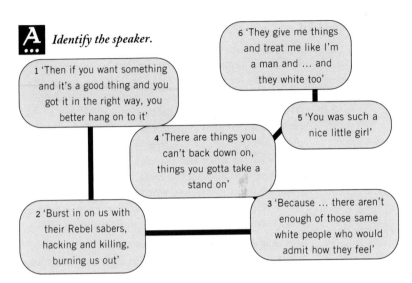

A *Identify the speaker.*

1 'Then if you want something and it's a good thing and you got it in the right way, you better hang on to it'

2 'Burst in on us with their Rebel sabers, hacking and killing, burning us out'

4 'There are things you can't back down on, things you gotta take a stand on'

6 'They give me things and treat me like I'm a man and ... and they white too'

5 'You was such a nice little girl'

3 'Because ... there aren't enough of those same white people who would admit how they feel'

Identify the person(s) 'to whom' this comment refers.

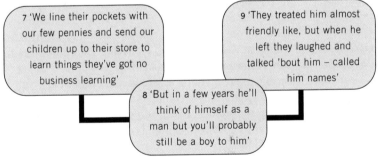

7 'We line their pockets with our few pennies and send our children up to their store to learn things they've got no business learning'

8 'But in a few years he'll think of himself as a man but you'll probably still be a boy to him'

9 'They treated him almost friendly like, but when he left they laughed and talked 'bout him – called him names'

Check your answers on page 80.

B *Consider these issues.*

a The likely effect of Uncle Hammer's words on Stacey.

b What the children learn from the stories they hear on Christmas Eve.

c The differing attitudes of white people towards black.

d The nature of the 'friendship' between T.J. and the Simms brothers.

e What the writer is showing us through Lillian Jean's lack of understanding of Cassie's actions.

f The growing tensions within society.

T.J. AND THE LAND

CHAPTER **10**

Papa is unable to return to the railroad and unwilling to let Uncle Hammer know of the family's financial difficulties for fear that he would seek revenge on the Wallaces. Mama is concerned for the welfare of Mr Morrison and feels it might be better if he leaves. The children accompany Mr Morrison to Mr Wiggin's place. On the way back Kaleb Wallace blocks their route with his truck and the children gaze in wonder as Mr Morrison picks up the truck and moves it off the road. Mama is even more worried when she hears that Kaleb Wallace threatened Mr Morrison but he asks to stay, explaining how much the family means to him.

Mr Morrison moves Kaleb Wallace's truck.

It is August and the children learn from Jeremy of white people who are pleased that their father has been hurt. T.J. is now spending much of his time with the Simms brothers and has, apparently, taken to stealing. Jeremy offers to show the others the tree he sleeps in at night, but Stacey declines the invitation. Mr Morrison returns from Strawberry with the news that the bank is calling in the loan, despite its having four more years to run. Knowing this is Harlan Granger's doing and yet unable to do anything else to save the land, Papa calls Uncle Hammer. He comes as soon as he can, arriving during the annual revival, and he has raised the money to clear the debt by selling his car. Papa is anxious that Uncle Hammer should return to Chicago as soon as the money is paid, fearing trouble if he tries to get back at the Wallaces.

In what ways does the tree house reflect Jeremy's isolation from white society?

The revival

A storm is brewing on the last night of the revival. T.J. arrives with the Simms brothers and Cassie notices that he is dressed more smartly than usual. He tells the Logan children that his new friends will give him anything he asks for, including a pearl-handled pistol. The children are not impressed by this and T.J. leaves to go to Strawberry with R.W. and Melvin.

COMMENT   Mr Morrison displays enormous physical strength lifting the truck. He also shows his loyalty to, and affection for, the family by persisting in his efforts to find work and saying how he would have liked a son and daughter like Mama and Papa.

Mr Granger creates more problems.   Harlan Granger's influence is demonstrated when the bank forecloses on the Logan's loan, showing how the white community sticks together when there is a hint of rebellion amongst the blacks. Papa explains this by saying, 'He's got a need to show us where we stand in the scheme of things' (p. 186).

The closeness of the black community is brought home in the portrayal of the revival, where every family, no matter how poor, manages to contribute something.

Hammer and the land   Uncle Hammer's true values become apparent when he sells the car to pay off the mortgage. The land is as important to him as it is to Papa and he is prepared to make sacrifices for it.

Whilst T.J. may have newer clothes, it is clear that the Simms brothers are not a good influence. He comes to the revival intending to show off, but finds that his old friends are not impressed by his material gains. At the end of this chapter he is a lonely and isolated figure, genuinely unable to understand what he has done wrong.

GLOSSARY   **ledger** accounts book
The bank called up the note the note is the mortgage on the land. By calling it up the bank is insisting that the Logans repay the debt immediately
revival religious festival intended to produce a reawakening of faith

CHAPTER **11**

To what extent It is a hot, unpleasant night with the threat of thunder
does the author use in the air. Cassie is disturbed by the arrival of T.J. who
the weather to is in great need of Stacey's help. Earlier that evening he
reflect significant had been with R.W. and Melvin when they tried to rob
events in the the Barnett mercantile. He originally thought they were
novel? simply going to get the gun he wanted so much and
was dismayed when he saw their faces masked with
stockings and watched them try to break into the safe.

The Barnett The robbery was disturbed by Mr Barnett and his wife,
robbery who were both injured in the ensuing struggle. T.J.
wanted to go home and threatened to tell on them if
they didn't take him. They beat him up badly and he
eventually made his own way back.

Despite Cassie's protests, Stacey decides to take T.J.
home and all the children go with him. Once they have
got him there they turn to head back, but are halted by
the sight of distant headlights. They watch silently as
The lynch mob T.J. and his family are dragged from the house and
arrives. beaten. Among his accusers are R.W. and Melvin who
claim to have seen him running away from the store
with two other black boys. T. J. is still carrying the gun
that was stolen from the store.

Mr Jamison calms Mr Jamison arrives on the scene with news that the
the mob. Barnetts are both alive and insists that the law should
decide whether or not T.J. is guilty. The men want to
lynch him straight away, but the sheriff stops them by
saying that Harlan Granger will have no lynching on
his land. So the men decide to hang him on the Logan
land and to get Mr Morrison and the children's father
at the same time. Stacey sends Cassie and the other
children back to the house to warn Papa and Mr
Morrison, insisting that he must stay to watch where
they take T.J. As the children hurry home the storm
breaks.

C OMMENT The chapter starts with lines of the blues song from
which the book derives its title. Its message is one of
defiance.

T.J.'s naivety T.J.'s vulnerability and naivety are clearly exposed. His
total inability to cope with what has happened –
including his foolish keeping of the gun – is in sharp
contrast to the cynical manoeuvres of the Simms
brothers. They ensured their faces were hidden during
the robbery, provided themselves with an alibi and were
first amongst T.J.'s accusers.

Ingrained Mrs Barnett's conviction that all the boys were black,
prejudice even though two had their faces hidden, says a great
deal about the extent of her prejudice. If T.J. is ever
tried in court she will be the main witness.

You see the night men through the eyes of the children
and observe the appalling and savage attack on the
Averys. The parents are dragged out by their feet, the
girls are slapped and spat upon and even 'quiet, gentle
Claude' is 'knocked to the ground and kicked' (p. 202).

Mr Jamison's intervention, in which he risks his own
life, contrasts starkly with Mr Granger's lack of interest.
The ambiguous message that there should be no

T.J. AND THE LAND

lynching on his land simply incites the men to move to the Logan land.

Stacey's courage and maturity are clearly demonstrated. He stands by his friend and has the good sense to send the other children home while he stays to watch in case the night men move on.

GLOSSARY   akimbo his elbow is turned outwards, his arm having been broken by Mr Morrison

a welling affirmation increasing agreement

CHAPTER 12

The children are in trouble when they first arrive home until they haltingly explain what has happened. Papa decides to go to T.J.'s house, despite Mama's objections, and Mr Morrison goes with him. The children sit and wait quietly, full of fear, until Mama

The cotton is on fire.

says that she smells smoke. Cassie realises that the cotton is on fire. Big Ma and Mama rush out to fight the fire, leaving the three children behind with strict instructions not to leave the house.

It is near dawn when Jeremy comes to the house and tells them that R.W., Melvin and many others have been fighting the fire throughout the night. The children are relieved to hear that Papa and Stacey are also there. What they really need is rain and as Jeremy

Rain quenches the flames.

turns to leave, he shouts excitedly that it is indeed raining. With dawn Cassie and Little Man set out to see what is happening, but Christopher John refuses to go with them. They watch as the firefighters wearily continue to dampen down the remaining patches of fire, only returning home when they see Big Ma and Mama approaching.

They learn that T.J. has been taken to Strawberry and that, because of the fire, further violence has been averted. Stacey reveals that Mr Morrison came to get him, making Cassie curious as to where her father had been. Mr Jamison visits with the news that Mr Barnett died that morning, and warns Papa not to get further

Cassie believes involved in T.J.'s case as others might become
that she can never suspicious about how the fire started. It is only then
speak about how that Cassie realises that her father had started the fire
the fire started. deliberately and with this realisation comes the
Why is this? knowledge that they can never talk about this, not even to each other.

Both Cassie and Stacey are deeply upset when Papa tells them that T.J. might be put on the chain gang or, worse still, executed for the killing of Mr Barnett. On hearing this Stacey runs into the forest and Cassie, after going to bed, starts to cry. She realises that her life will go on as it always has, but that T.J.'s has changed forever. She does not understand what happened in the night and she cries for both T.J. and the land.

COMMENT   Papa does not hesitate to risk his life by going to help his neighbours. He sees the night's events as the culmination of the recent build up of racial tension in the area.

Dependency on Papa starts the fire knowing this would be the only way
cotton brings to divert attention from T.J. The white and black
whites and blacks communities are united in their efforts to douse the
together. flames as they are all dependent on the cotton crop for their livelihoods. Even Mr Granger is seen fighting the fire.

Christopher John has, up to this point, always followed the lead of his brothers and sister. For the first time he refuses to do their bidding by staying at the family home and both Cassie and Little Man are amazed by this.

With the news of Mr Barnett's death, Papa knows that

T.J. AND THE LAND

things look bad for T.J. He does not seek to hide this from his children, believing they have a right to the truth even though it will upset them.

Cassie cries for T.J. and the land. At the end of the story Cassie cries for both T.J. and the land. Although she had never particularly liked T.J. he was part of her life, and more particularly of her childhood. Now he has been taken away unfairly. She cries for the land which is so dear to her family, knowing that her father has just destroyed a quarter of the cotton crop in his efforts to save T.J.

GLOSSARY   **bolls** rounded capsules containing the seeds of the cotton plant

TEST YOURSELF (Chapters 10–12)

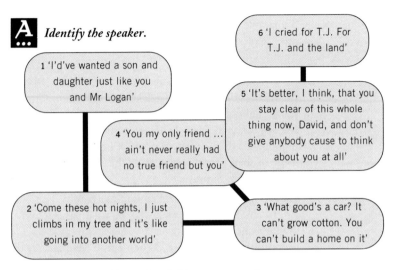

A *Identify the speaker.*

1 'I'd've wanted a son and daughter just like you and Mr Logan'

2 'Come these hot nights, I just climbs in my tree and it's like going into another world'

3 'What good's a car? It can't grow cotton. You can't build a home on it'

4 'You my only friend ... ain't never really had no true friend but you'

5 'It's better, I think, that you stay clear of this whole thing now, David, and don't give anybody cause to think about you at all'

6 'I cried for T.J. For T.J. and the land'

Identify the person(s) 'to whom' this comment refers.

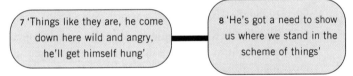

7 'Things like they are, he come down here wild and angry, he'll get himself hung'

8 'He's got a need to show us where we stand in the scheme of things'

Check your answers on page 80.

B *Consider these issues.*

a Whether Papa's concerns for Uncle Hammer are justified by his actions.

b Why Mr Morrison becomes so attached to the Logan family.

c The importance of friendship in the story as a whole.

d Why Mr Granger fails to take any direct action to prevent the proposed lynching.

e Why the writer portrays violence against the entire Avery family.

f What might have happened had Papa not set fire to the cotton when he did.

g The images of white people presented by Mr Jamison and Jeremy.

h How your feelings towards T.J. have changed by the end of the story.

47

COMMENTARY

THEMES

THE FAMILY — In writing this book Mildred Taylor said she 'wanted to show a family united in love and self-respect'. The Logans are such a family, their positive qualities highlighted by the marked contrast between them and some of their neighbours such as the Averys or, more strikingly, the Simmses.

Cassie — Cassie's young life revolves around her family. The Logan children have been raised, by their parents and grandmother, to stand by each other and to give support when it is needed. When Little Man refuses his book at school, Cassie also refuses hers. When Cassie is insulted by Mr Barnett at the Mercantile, Stacey is angry on her behalf. When Stacey insists on taking T.J. home the other children insist on going too.

The land — The family work together picking the cotton crop and are taught to take pride in their land, their name and their heritage. The children all know the story of the land and are aware that they must make sacrifices for its sake. They have a strong sense of family identity and of being privileged relative to their neighbours. When Stacey complains about Mr Avery and Mr Lanier withdrawing from the shopping in Vicksburg Papa quickly reminds him that he was 'born blessed' (p. 165) with land of his own.

Mama and Papa — Mama and Papa are portrayed as ideal parents. They provide a loving and caring environment for their children, as is clearly illustrated in the Christmas scene. They are strict when the need arises, believing in physical punishment as a positive method of dealing with disobedience. More frequently they discuss difficulties with their children and it is to the parents

Y

that the children turn when they need advice. Papa is consulted by Cassie about Lillian Jean and by Stacey about Jeremy. The parents are also supportive of each other, demonstrating consideration, love and mutual respect. When Mama loses her job it is Papa who comforts her. When she objects to his proposed visit to Strawberry it is through genuine concern for his safety. They teach their children through example. When Papa goes to the aid of T.J. he says, 'I'll do what I have to do, Mary ... and so will you' (p. 208), thus demonstrating their joint approach to life, an approach which their children are rapidly learning.

The Averys   The Averys are presented in contrast to the Logan family. They sharecrop on Mr Granger's land and, in consequence, are poorer and lack financial independence. They also clearly care for their children and want to set a good example to them. Mr Avery agrees to shop in Vicksburg and only stops when put under extreme pressure by Mr Granger and the Wallaces. When T.J. is attacked by the night men both Mr and Mrs Avery do their best to protect him and their love for their wayward son is evident in this scene. Mildred Taylor does, however, seem to be critical of them as parents in as much as they have not kept sufficiently strict control over T.J. This sentiment is voiced by Mama in Chapter 9 when she criticises Mr and Mrs Avery for failing in their responsibility as parents by allowing T.J. to behave as he does. Though Papa defends them by saying that they lack the physical strength to punish him, you understand – recalling how T.J. allowed Claude to take the blame when he went to the Wallace store – that he has been allowed to get away with too much for too long.

The Simmses   The only white family explored in any detail is the Simms family. You are shown the four children and the father. It is a curious family, with Jeremy clearly not fitting in or accepting the dictates of a racist and bullying father. He seeks out the company of the Logan children and is isolated within his own family. When Jeremy tells Cassie he will be lonely when she and her brothers finish school she finds it difficult to understand. 'Lonely?' she says, 'With all them brothers and sisters you got?' (p. 159). His sister Lillian Jean has never questioned, as he has, what she has been taught about white superiority. She is, therefore, genuinely confused when Cassie attacks her in the wood and, to some extent, can be seen as a victim of the views with which she has been indoctrinated from a young age. At the other extreme, Melvin and R.W. behave in an abominable way towards T.J., cynically ensuring that he is blamed for the crime they have committed. Clearly they follow the example of their father, a man prepared to bully and physically abuse Cassie in order to stress his daughter's social superiority.

Other families

Other families appear only briefly in the story. Moe Turner's father sets a good example by encouraging his son to make the long trek to school every day and he is willing to shop in Vicksburg if Mama can find someone to back the credit. The Jamisons, another family that are worthy of respect, work together and discuss important issues. Mr Jamison makes it clear that he and his wife have talked about the problems they will face in agreeing to back the credit. Mr Granger's grandmother is shown as having had a negative effect on her grandson. She instilled in him a strong sense of family but with the result that he 'lived in the past' (p. 134) and was unable to adapt to, and resentful of, the changes wrought by the Civil War. The Wallaces are rarely referred to individually, but as a group they demonstrate racism at its very worst, being prepared to burn and murder black people if they feel they are asserting themselves.

THE COMMUNITY

There are in reality two communities, the black and the white. They are divided by their history, their culture and above all by their colour. The children go to different schools and the adults do not mix socially. Interaction between the two is frowned upon, as shown by Papa when he advises Stacey against developing a friendship with Jeremy, and it is through his 'friendship' with the Simms brothers that T.J. is led astray and ultimately ruined.

The black community

The Logan family are part of a black community which is portrayed as being mutually supportive. They are generous to those outside their family, welcoming Mr Morrison into their home and providing hospitality for the large Avery family at Christmas time. Big Ma shares her knowledge of medicines with the Berrys, Mama drives for almost two hours to visit them and Papa does not stop to think of the danger when he hastens to help the Averys. The Logans assume a prominent role within the community by seeking to persuade others not to allow their children to go to the Wallace store and by organising the shopping trips to Vicksburg.

The black community is a close one where people work to help each other, an example being the funding given to the school by the black church. Religion also provides a framework for social occasions in the community. The importance of food in a poor rural area is made clear both at the revival, where every family – no matter how badly off – contributes something, and at the Logan's Christmas celebrations.

The white community

In contrast, we see no similar images of the white community. The Simms and Wallace families are shown only in their interactions with black people, most of which are unpleasant. They are united only in their shared racist views. Mr Jamison and Jeremy are the exceptions. Jeremy provides a note of hope for the future, but he is lonely and isolated within his family and the white community, a situation reflected in his desire to live in a tree house.

The communities unite

At the end of the story the two communities are united in their fight against the fire. Mr Lanier and Mr Simms work side by side 'each oblivious of the other' (p. 214). The need of the whites to subjugate the blacks is overridden by a stronger need and there is irony in the fact that they can work in harmony and for the common good. You should be wary, however, of seeing this as a scene of reconciliation, for it is made very clear that T.J. will still be tried and almost certainly found guilty of a crime he did not commit.

RACISM

The concept of colour lies at the heart of the novel. Black citizens living in Mississippi in the 1930s had few rights, virtually no recourse to the law and were, at times, subject to extreme violence from their white neighbours. The legacy of slavery was ever present. Through Cassie, a young child, you are shown the terrible consequences of racism and share her growing perception of its unfairness and bigotry.

Growing up with racism

Initially you see the effects of racism on the immediate lives of the Logan children. They have to walk to school while the white children have a bus. Once there, the provision made for them is pitiful by comparison, and they have to endure humiliations such as using books considered unfit for white children. The Logan children, however, follow the example of their parents by not simply accepting things as they are and by taking direct action wherever possible, for instance when they strand the school bus.

The adult world

As the story progresses you are made increasingly aware of the adult world and the effects of racism in it. The

Berrys are badly burned, Sam Tatum is tarred and feathered, the Wallaces are not charged with murder and the black community is not free to shop where it chooses. Gradually the worlds of adult and child merge, as T.J. becomes increasingly involved with the Simms brothers and is ultimately wrongly charged with the murder of Mr Barnett. Throughout the story the night men are a threatening presence in the background, representing lawlessness and racial hatred at its worst.

Some white characters show no prejudice.

Amongst the white characters (see Literary Terms), only Mr Jamison and Jeremy exhibit no prejudice and you are given some insight into the thoughts and motivations of both these characters. Elsewhere in the novel you see just the effects of prejudice and not the reasons for it. To this extent most of the white characters are simply representations of an idea. The consequences of their actions are shown, but not the thoughts, feelings or motives that incite them.

Not all white characters are bad, nor all black characters good. Miss Crocker is shown to be self-righteous and lacking in understanding of the fundamental issues of racism believing – almost as Lillian Jean does – that there is no need to question the way things are. T.J., though not inherently bad, is shown to be foolish, easily led and cowardly. He does not, however, deserve the fate that awaits him.

EDUCATION

Mama and Papa value their children's education.

Mama is set apart from many of the other black characters by her education. Her father made many sacrifices for this, believing it to be extremely important. The Logan children are brought up with a respect for education and much of their time at home is spent in study. They are given books for Christmas and Papa takes great pride in the fact that his children are able to read the difficult texts. Little Man treats his book with reverent awe. Cassie does not like school, but the reason for this is that she is bored and uninspired by Miss Crocker's teaching.

Inequalities in education

Black children do not have equality of opportunity in education, perhaps not surprising given the limited resources made available by the state. The school curriculum, however – determined by a white School Board – is another major factor in this lack of equality. The children are taught a version of history – and in particular of slavery – which, according to Mama, is not true. The few reading books they have only contain pictures of white children and bear little relevance to the lives of the black children. This almost certainly reflects Mildred Taylor's own experience, in which she recognised a 'terrible contradiction' between what she was told at school and what she had learnt at home.

A positive force

Education is certainly promoted as a positive force in the lives of young blacks. Even T.J. recognises the significance of passing his end of year exams, having already failed them once. He is not interested, however, in working to achieve the results he needs and is prepared to cheat instead. This negative quality is in strong contrast to the attitude of Moe, who is prepared to walk for many hours each day to get an education.

ECONOMIC FREEDOM

The Logans have economic freedom – up to a point.

The Logans have greater economic independence than the rest of their black neighbours and this is one of the main themes (see Literary Terms) of the story. Unlike the Averys and the Laniers, the Logans have a certain amount of freedom and choice in their lives. Papa is free to shop in Vicksburg, but he needs the backing of Mr Jamison as guarantor to enable his neighbours to join him. Even with this backing some of the sharecroppers are completely at the mercy of the plantation owners. Mr Lanier and Mr Avery have to withdraw from the scheme when Mr Granger threatens to cut the percentage they are paid from the cotton crop. Furthermore, the Wallaces are going to call in the money owed to them and the sharecroppers run the risk of being put on the chain gang if they fail to honour their debts.

An economic system for whites

The entire economic system is controlled by the whites, giving them enormous power over the blacks. The fact that the Logan's loan has four years to run is of no consequence when Mr Granger decides he wants to make life difficult for them. It is easy for Mr Granger to influence the manager of the First National Bank and even if Papa did take the matter to court he would be unlikely to win his case. We have already seen how little attention the law pays to the blacks.

Were it not for Uncle Hammer the Logans would be in serious trouble. He is in a position to sell his car and pay off the loan, but it is made clear that he could never have got to this position if he had stayed in the South. There, wages are pitifully low, the top price for any day's labour being fifty cents. Uncle Hammer is resented by the whites because he has escaped the economic stranglehold of the South and is clearly successful and prosperous.

VIOLENCE IN SOCIETY

The story is set against a background of racial hatred and violence which permeates the lives of all. Predominantly the violence is of whites against blacks but this is not always the case. In the early stages of the story we learn of the brutal burning of the Berrys. At this point the Logan children seem to have little comprehension of the enormity of this abuse, only fully grasping it when Mama decides to take them to see Mr Berry and show them at first hand the terrible disfigurement and suffering that has been inflicted upon him. The fear of the night men, however, is never far

The burning of the Berrys

The night men

from their minds and they are convinced that they will be made to suffer for having damaged the white children's bus. They are relieved to learn that it was not them but Sam Tatum that the night men were looking for. Yet again they seem to have only a tentative grasp of what it means to be tarred and feathered. The final chapters of the story are filled with violence, starting with the attack on the Barnetts by the Simms brothers and culminating in the savage attack on the Avery family by the night men. By this stage the children have had first hand experience of violence through the unprovoked attack on Stacey, Papa and Mr Morrison on the way back from Vicksburg. The children see the assault on T.J. and his family and you witness it through Cassie's young eyes. Mildred Taylor clearly detests this pointless violence and conveys this strongly throughout *Roll of Thunder, Hear My Cry*.

Acceptable violence?

There are times, though, when violence is acceptable, or at least understandable. When Mr Morrison retaliates against the Wallace brothers, he inflicts grievous injuries on them. This is justified, however, as self-defence, it being made clear to you that Stacey and Papa would have had little chance of survival if Mr Morrison had not been there. The situation is not as clear cut when Cassie attacks Lillian Jean or, for that matter, when the children damage the white children's school bus. Whilst you may enjoy Cassie's revenge for the humiliation she suffered in Strawberry, the author deliberately diminishes her triumph by showing Lillian Jean to be both confused and genuinely upset by Cassie's actions. It is clear that, while violence may be acceptable as a last resort, it is not recommended as a constructive way of resolving differences.

STRUCTURE

Chronological order The structure (see Literary Terms) of this novel is relatively simple. Events are described in chronological order, that is, in the order in which they happen. The story follows a single, but very significant, year in the life of Cassie Logan, starting in October at the beginning of the school year. By Chapter 3 it is the end of October and by Chapter 7 Christmas is being celebrated. Spring arrives in Chapter 9 and the story moves rapidly on to August by Chapter 10, ending with Cassie thinking ahead to starting school in October in Chapter 12.

The role of the weather The progress of the seasons is matched by the changing weather, which provides an important part of the story's backdrop. At the start the weather is dry and the earth warm, but the red dust turns to mud as heavy rains fall and the children are soaked on their way to school. By Christmas it is cold, with the family gathering round a warm fire. Stacey needs a good warm coat to keep the chill out. Spring arrives in early March 'Rain-drenched, fresh, vital, full of life' (p. 158), heralding the end of the **The revival** school year. On the night of the revival in August, 'the air felt close, suffocating, and no wind stirred' (p. 190). A storm is brewing but it does not actually break until much later that night, when the children are rushing home to tell their parents about the danger that threatens them. It is much later still when the rain actually falls and helps the firefighters quench the flames that threaten to engulf the cotton.

Whilst this event forms the climax to the entire novel, it is not the only time that dangerous or menacing events are linked to stormy weather. On the day the children dig the gully to strand the Jefferson Davis bus the 'thunder rolled across the sky' (p. 43) and on the night Papa, Mr Morrison and Stacey are attacked on their way back from Strawberry, it rains heavily and the thunder rumbles overhead.

The changes in the weather and the passage of the seasons form the background to the gradual build-up of racial tension in the area, which you see through the eyes of a young girl who is herself only beginning to gain an insight into the society in which she lives. Things are already unsettled at the start of the story, as is shown by the burning of the Berrys and then the tarring and feathering of Sam Tatum.

Logans are a natural target for white hatred.

Increasingly the Logans become a natural target for the dislike of the white people, partly because they possess their own land, but also because they refuse to be put down. Uncle Hammer is delighted to show off his car, which is a newer model than the one owned by Mr Granger, and Mama refuses to accept the version of history recommended by the School Board even though it means she will lose her job. By the time Papa makes his fateful trip to Strawberry feelings are running very high. When Mr Morrison physically moves Kaleb Wallace's truck off the road, Wallace cries out in hatred 'One of these nights, you watch, nigger! I'm gonna come get you for what you done!' (p. 181). Papa is right when he says 'This thing's been coming a long time' (p. 207) and that T.J. just happened to be the one who *Adult and child* 'triggered' it. The whole book leads up to this *worlds unite.* culmination of racial hatred and the unification of the worlds of the adult and the child.

CHARACTERS

CASSIE

The narrator
Nine years old
Bright
Sensitive
Quick tempered
Determined
Hates injustice

Cassie is the central character (see Literary Terms) of the story. You see events through her eyes and share her experiences and growing awareness of the unfairness and injustice of the society in which she lives. She is a lively, clever, animated nine year old girl with a strong sense of self-worth and a fiery temper, which her father likens to Uncle Hammer's.

Her family is the centre of her existence and she has a close and caring relationship with her three brothers. When Little Man refuses to accept his book at school, Cassie refuses to accept hers, even though it means that she will get the switch. When Stacey insists on taking T.J. home, Cassie will not let him go alone, regardless of it being late and possibly dangerous. She looks to her parents for guidance on important matters, respecting their opinions above all others. It is important to her that her mother should understand why she and Little Man refused their books and when she realises that Mama does she is no longer worried. When she is humiliated by Lillian Jean, she waits for an opportunity to talk to her father before acting and his advice clearly influences the action that she does take.

In the course of the story Cassie begins to learn that things are not always as they should be. It is a lesson which, though painful, is ultimately essential to her survival. She experiences personal fear when confronted with the night men, who she thinks are seeking revenge for the damage done to the bus, and she witnesses the terrible consequences of their actions when her mother takes her to see Mr Berry. In Strawberry she learns the painful lesson that sometimes unfairness must be borne. Just as Big Ma has to set up her stall at the back of the field, so Cassie has to apologise to Lillian Jean. As her mother explains to her, 'It happened and you have to accept that in the world outside this house, things are not always as we would have them to be' (p. 105). The

greatest injustice of all comes, however, towards the end
of the story. Cassie has never liked T.J. but he has
always been part of her life. She watches as he is badly
beaten by the white mob for a crime he did not
commit, the real culprits standing amongst his accusers,
and she must accept the possibility that he may yet face
the death penalty. A part of her young life will never be
the same again and it is this knowledge that brings the
tears to her eyes in the closing pages of the story.

STACEY
Cassie's brother
Twelve years old
Tolerant
Protective of his
siblings
Courageous
A true friend

At twelve he is three years older than Cassie and has a
much broader understanding of the way things are.
Like Cassie, he is angered by Mr Barnett's behaviour in
the store and knows that was it wrong. Yet he also
knows enough about the world to get Cassie out as
quickly as he can, telling her, 'I know it and you know
it, but he don't know it, and that's where the trouble is'
(p. 95). He has a strong sense of family and when Little
Man is so upset about the bus that he starts to cry, it is
Stacey who takes the initiative and leads the others in a
plan to get even. He regards himself as the man of the
family when his father is away and it is for this reason
that he at first resents the presence of Mr Morrison.
Stacey has, however, many lessons to learn. He, along
with Cassie, is taken to see Mr Berry so that he will
know why his parents have ordered him not to go to
the Wallace store. His father takes him to Vicksburg
because he wants Stacey to know 'a man's things'
and 'how to handle himself' (p. 167). During the
fire Stacey is working with the adults to put out
the flames.

It is through his relationship with T.J., however, that
Stacey has most to learn. He is at first friendly with
T.J., tolerating his behaviour and generally overlooking
his 'underhanded stunts' (p. 15). He is angered by his
attempts to cheat in the school exams but, nevertheless,

takes the blame when caught by his mother with T.J.'s notes. He is clearly influenced by T.J. in the early stages of the story, no more so than when he gives him the brand new coat which was a present from Uncle Hammer. He does, however, learn from his mistake. When T.J. taunts him about the wooden flute that Jeremy gave him for Christmas he retaliates quickly saying, 'Ah, stuff it, T.J.' (p. 129). He continues to be friends with T.J., but is clearly more wary of him. When T.J. directly hurts a member of his family – by causing his mother to lose her job – he refuses to have anything more to do with him. He has not stopped caring, however, and when T.J. needs help to get home Stacey does not hesitate to give it and bravely stays to watch when the night men arrive. He is deeply upset by the thought that T.J. may die and at the end of the story rushes into the forest 'his eyes filled with heavy tears' (pp. 219-20).

T.J. AVERY

Stacey's friend
Foolish
Selfish
Easily led

He is two years older than Stacey and has returned to school because he failed his exams the previous year. His father, a sharecropper, is a sickly man who is finding it increasingly difficult to discipline his son. In the early stages of the story T.J. is presented as a foolish youth willing to cheat in exams and one who has no conscience about getting either his brother or his best friend into trouble. You see him mainly through Cassie's eyes and she states very clearly that she does not like him. It is worth remembering, however, that T.J. is Stacey's friend. Whilst he may be very foolish and unable to accept the consequences of his own actions, he is not portrayed as being bad. Mildred Taylor seems to attribute many of his problems to weak parenting, a thought expressed by Mama when she says, 'It's just that the boy's gotten out of hand, and doesn't seem like anybody's doing anything about it' (p. 167). When he loses the friendship of the Logan children,

Lacking
confidence
Wants to impress
Vulnerable
A victim

T.J. loses his place in the community and turns to the Simms brothers for companionship. You sense that despite his boasting about his new white friends who give him everything he wants, T.J. is nevertheless aware that they are an inadequate substitute for Stacey. When he attends the revival he hopes to impress the other children, but instead is left a lonely and isolated figure for whom even Cassie feels sorry.

T.J. is terrified by the events at the Barnett store and you are encouraged to feel sympathy both for the physical injuries inflicted on him and for his initial inability to grasp the seriousness of his situation. His main concern is to get back home so that his father will not throw him out as he has no other place to go. He does not even have the sense to get rid of the pistol which has got him into so much trouble. He is like a child when he calls Stacey his only 'true friend' (p. 199) and even Cassie is made aware of T.J.'s 'vulnerability'. T.J. may be a foolish youth but he is loved by his parents who risk their own lives in trying to save him from the lynch mob. There is little hope offered for T.J. at the end of the story. As Papa tells the children, he faces either the chain gang or execution. It is a harsh reality, but one with which Mildred Taylor wants to confront her readers.

MAMA

The Logan
children's mother
Educated
A teacher
Strict
Loving
Resists racism
Brave
Supportive of her
family

The children's mother and a teacher in their school, Mama is the guiding force in their lives. Her father had made her education a main priority and 'every penny he'd get his hands on he'd put it aside for her schooling' (p. 152). She is different to the other teachers in the school and regarded by many as a 'disrupting maverick' (p. 30), her ideas being considered too radical. She refuses to simply accept things as they are, covering over the offensive fronts of the school books and teaching the children a different version of history to

y

that endorsed by the School Board. She is strict with her children, disciplining them when they are disobedient but listening when they have troubles. The children love and respect her and accept her punishments. In her dealings with her children she is always fair and consistent, helping them develop a strong sense of family and self-worth. When Cassie is upset about the incident at Strawberry, Mama takes time to explain the prejudices that underlie racist attitudes. She ends with the positive message that 'what we do have is some choice over what we make of our lives once we're here' (p. 107).

For much of the time Papa is away and Mama is responsible, with Big Ma, for the running of the household. It is she who visits the neighbours to canvass support for the shopping trip to Vicksburg, believing not only that the Wallaces are 'bad people' but that they have a corrupting influence on young blacks. She is more cautious than Papa, however, urging him not to go when there is danger. Her concern proves to be justified when Papa is attacked and ends up with a broken leg and a bullet wound.

PAPA
The Logan children's father
Works on the railroad
Caring
Thoughtful
Stands up for his beliefs

Initially Papa plays only a small part in the action of the story, making an appearance in Chapter 2 – when he arrives with Mr Morrison – and then not returning to the family home until Chapter 7. Though he is spoken of by the other characters (see Literary Terms) it is only at this point that he becomes a major figure in the plot. Like Mama, he is portrayed as a good parent who loves his children and wants the best for them. He has a strong sense of family and constantly stresses the importance of the land to the children. Early in the story Cassie recalls how her father 'never divided the land in his mind; it was simply Logan land' (p. 12). When Stacey criticises Mr Avery and Mr Lanier, Papa is quick to remind him that he was 'born blessed' (p. 165) because he has land of his own. He compares his family to a fig tree which has deep roots and continues to flourish year after year.

His children seek his advice and attend to what he says. Cassie asks for his opinion before deciding on what course of action to take with Lillian Jean and Stacey, on hearing his father's doubts about the possibility of sustaining a friendship with Jeremy, carefully puts the flute away in his box of treasured possessions. Papa takes pride in his children's achievements, but does not hesitate to punish them when they have disobeyed him, as when they go to the Wallace store. He is anxious that Stacey should not go astray like T.J. and tries to avoid this by giving Stacey the additional responsibility of accompanying him to Vicksburg. He believes, like Mama, that they should not simply accept things the way they are and is conscious that in making a stand about the Wallaces they are setting a positive example to their children. He says, 'I want these children to know we tried, and what we can't do now, maybe one day they will' (p. 135).

Papa's leg is broken in the attack on the way back from Vicksburg, preventing him from returning to work on the railroad. Though his instinct is to get revenge, he has the sense to realise that this would lead to further trouble. He differs from his brother Hammer in that he is more cautious and restrained, qualities which enable him to diffuse the potentially tragic situation that befalls T.J. He does not hesitate to help his neighbours in their distress and shows great courage and presence of mind in his decision to set the cotton alight. With his wife he leads his children by example, and the love and respect they feel for him is evident throughout the story.

UNCLE HAMMER

Papa's younger brother

Works in the North

Quick tempered

Rash

Loves the land

Sense of justice

Uncle Hammer is Big Ma's youngest surviving son. Though he does not play a large part in the action of the story, he is an important character for several reasons. Papa compares Cassie to her Uncle Hammer when he speaks of her quick temper. Unable to stand the discrimination and pitifully low wages of the southern states, he has moved to the North where he can earn a good living, dress smartly and own a brand new Packard. To the children he is something of a hero, though Cassie says that he is more distant than their father. He spoils them with presents but can be ruthless when there is a lesson to be taught. When Stacey gives his coat to T. J. his uncle will not allow the coat to be returned, saying that Stacey must learn to hold on to things that are rightfully his. He has a fiery temper, shown when he hears of the humiliation suffered by Cassie at the hands of Lillian Jean in Strawberry. Were it not for Mr Morrison he would almost certainly have gone to the Simms' house and could have ended up in serious trouble. It is because of his temper that Papa will not tell him of his broken leg and only goes to him for the money for the mortgage when there is nowhere else to turn.

Uncle Hammer may have left his childhood home behind but his heart is still firmly rooted in the land. Understanding its importance to the family, he does not hesitate to sell his car in order to pay off the debt. There is, however, clearly no place for him in the racist environment of Mississippi, where he is resented for his prosperity, and he returns to the North well before the story reaches its conclusion.

BIG MA
Mother of Papa
and Hammer
Hard working
Capable
Caring
Perceptive

Big Ma is a background figure for much of the story, only occasionally taking a more prominent role. She is the children's paternal grandmother and clearly sees it as her responsibility that they should be fully aware of their family history. Cassie is happy to listen to her stories about the trees and the land, though she already knows the details well. Big Ma has worked hard all her life and suffered the loss of several children, but she is proud of what she has achieved and is determined that the family should keep the land. She signs it over to her sons to ensure there are no problems when she dies.

She contributes much to the domestic life of the family and continues to work in the cotton fields. Though she is strict with the children and 'not one for coddling' them (p. 42), she offers comfort when they need it, as when Little Man is upset about his clothes. She is clearly distressed at having to make Cassie apologise to Lillian Jean in Strawberry, but has the wisdom to realise that this is the best course of action. At the close of the story she does not hesitate to join Mama in fighting the fire and when she returns home after an exhausting night her first thoughts are for T.J.'s mother, who she immediately goes to visit.

MINOR CHARACTERS

MR GRANGER

He has many things in common with Mr Jamison, in that he is from the 'Old South' and had a college education. He holds, however, very different views to him and has been strongly influenced by his grandmother's stories of 'the glory of the South before the war' (p. 134). He resents the fact that the Logans own land that once belonged to his family and will not countenance any suggestion of equality for the blacks. He is a man of influence and power and uses this to get the bank to foreclose on the Logans' loan. He has the opportunity to stop the proposed lynching of T.J. but instead sends the ambiguous message that he will not stand for any hanging on his land, the implication being that he has no objection if they go elsewhere.

MR JAMISON

He is a lawyer in Strawberry and is much liked by the Logan children because he treats their parents with respect. In the story he is representative of a minority of whites who do not approve of the injustices in the society, nor of the way the blacks are treated. He is willing to stand by his beliefs, backing the credit of the sharecropping families who agree to shop at Vicksburg. He is, however, a realist and warns Papa that ultimately they won't win against the powerful landowners such as Mr Granger.

When the mob are threatening to lynch T.J. he intervenes, risking his own life by doing so. He knows that Papa set fire to the cotton to avert the crisis and it is clear from his friendly warning to Papa that he approves of what he has done.

MR MORRISON

Mr Morrison is brought home by Papa to take care of the family. He is a huge man and has enormous strength, demonstrated when he fights the Wallace brothers and later when he lifts the truck off the road. He was born of slaves who were bred for their physical strength and on Christmas Eve describes how his family were slaughtered by the night men some fifty years before. He is generally reserved, though in the course of the story he comes to look on the Logans as his family.

JEREMY SIMMS

Jeremy is the young white boy who befriends the Logan children. He is ostracised and bullied by his sister Lillian Jean because of this. Jeremy is a misfit who is unable to accept the prejudices of the society in which he lives. Much to Stacey's surprise, he does not like his brothers and sisters very much. He also has a difficult relationship with his father and is unable to tell him about visiting the Logans on Christmas Day. Jeremy is alienated from his family, something which is highlighted by his desire to live in a tree house. He has insight and understanding beyond his years and offers some hope for a better future.

LITTLE MAN

The youngest of the Logan children, he is also, perhaps, the most sensitive. He is outraged when his clothes are dirtied on the way to school and delighted to help his brothers and sister execute their revenge. Though only six years old, he is not afraid to stand up for what he believes and refuses to accept the book at school because of its offensive label.

CHRISTOPHER JOHN

He is the mildest and quietest of the Logan children and is the one most eager to please others. He does not want to join the others in the digging of the trench, nor in going to the Wallace store, but does so rather than be left on his own. He gains in confidence as the story progresses, speaking out firmly against T.J. for the hurt he caused Mama and refusing to join Cassie and Little Man when they go to take a closer look at the fire.

CLAUDE

Claude is T.J.'s younger brother and a friend of the Logan children. He is a gentle and passive character who is bullied by T.J. and kicked by the night men.

R.W. AND MELVIN

The two Simms brothers are not depicted separately in the story. They 'befriend' T.J. whilst laughing at him behind his back. It is they who are responsible for the petty thefts and for the injuries to the Barnetts when the robbery goes wrong. They escape punishment for this by blaming T. J. and two other black boys.

THE WALLACES

The Wallaces are virtually indistinguishable as individuals. As a group they represent the worst of the southern white culture. They set fire to the Berrys, corrupt the young blacks and attack the Logans. They escape punishment from the law and are hugely offended when Mr Morrison gives them a dose of their own medicine.

LANGUAGE & STYLE

The story is narrated by Cassie in a first person narrative (see Literary Terms). This technique gives the author the opportunity to enlist your sympathies and show you things in a particular way. It has its drawbacks, however, and can lead to contrived situations such as overheard, reported adult conversations. At times it is the adult voice that is prominent, as at the end when Cassie reflects on the fate of T.J.

In speech Cassie uses rough local dialect (see Literary Terms), but her thoughts and observations are conveyed through a more formal or standardised English. This can lead to interesting contrasts, for example, '"Shoot", I mumbled finally, unable to restrain from further comment, "it ain't my fault you gotta be in Mama's class this year"' (p. 10). Most of the characters use the local dialect with no clear distinction being made between black or white, adult or child. Thus we find Mr Simms saying, 'Not 'fore she 'pologizes to my gal, y'all ain't' (p. 97). The author helps you to imagine the actual sound of the words chiefly by shortening words and frequent use of the apostrophe. This is clearly evident in this sample of T.J.'s speech: 'I betcha I could give y'all an earful 'bout that burnin' last night' (p. 13).

Exceptions to this pattern can be found in the language of Mama and Mr Jamison, both of whom have been educated. Their speech is more formal and grammatically correct. The contrast is shown when Cassie says to her mother, 'Ah, shoot! White ain't nothin'!' and her mother replies, 'White is something just like black is something' (p. 105). Mr Granger, who also has a college education, speaks in a 'folksy dialect', the implication being that he consciously chooses to do so.

Sometimes more stylised language is used for particular effect. When Mr Morrison is describing the violence of the Christmas of 1876, his speech is littered with Biblical imagery. He tells how the 'devlish' night men 'swept down like locusts' and how his family 'fought them demons out of hell like avenging angels of the Lord' (pp. 122-3). At times the narrative is full of imagery, as when Cassie describes the arrival of the night men. She sees 'a caravan of headlights ... like cat eyes in the night' which, as they retreat, are like 'distant red embers' (p. 59). The Moon is 'cloaking' the earth and Mr Morrison is moving like a 'jungle cat'. When Papa is explaining to Cassie about the importance of the family he uses the image of the fig tree.

STUDY SKILLS

HOW TO USE QUOTATIONS

One of the secrets of success in writing essays is the
way you use quotations. There are five basic principles:
- Put inverted commas at the beginning and end of the
  quotation
- Write the quotation exactly as it appears in the
  original
- Do not use a quotation that repeats what you have
  just written
- Use the quotation so that it fits into your sentence
- Keep the quotation as short as possible

Quotations should be used to develop the line of
thought in your essays.

Your comment should not duplicate what is in your
quotation. For example:

> Cassie tells us that the day in Strawberry was the cruellest she
> had ever faced, 'No day in all my life had ever been as cruel as
> this one'.

Far more effective is to write:

> When telling us of her experience in Strawberry, Cassie says,
> 'No day in all my life had ever been as cruel as this one'.

However, the most sophisticated way of using the
writer's words is to embed them into your sentence:

> Cassie reveals the awfulness of her experience in Strawberry
> when she says she has never faced a day 'as cruel as this one'.

When you use quotations in this way, you are
demonstrating the ability to use text as evidence to
support your ideas - not simply including words from
the original to prove you have read it.

Everyone writes differently. Work through the suggestions given here and adapt the advice to suit your own style and interests. This will improve your essay writing skills and allow your personal voice to emerge.

The following points indicate in ascending order the skills of essay writing:
- Picking out one or two facts about the story and adding the odd detail
- Writing about the text by retelling the story
- Retelling the story and adding a quotation here and there
- Organising an answer which explains what is happening in the text and giving quotations to support what you write
....
- Writing in such a way as to show that you have thought about the intentions of the writer of the text and that you understand the techniques used
- Writing at some length, giving your viewpoint on the text and commenting by picking out details to support your views
- Looking at the text as a work of art, demonstrating clear critical judgement and explaining to the reader of your essay how the enjoyment of the text is assisted by literary devices, linguistic effects and psychological insights; showing how the text relates to the time when it was written

The dotted line above represents the division between lower and higher level grades. Higher level performance begins when you start to consider your response as a reader of the text. The highest level is reached when you offer an enthusiastic personal response and show how this piece of literature is a product of its time.

Coursework essay

Set aside an hour or so at the start of your work to plan what you have to do.

- List all the points you feel are needed to cover the task. Collect page references of information and quotations that will support what you have to say. A helpful tool is the highlighter pen: this saves painstaking copying and enables you to target precisely what you want to use.
- Focus on what you consider to be the main points of the essay. Try to sum up your argument in a single sentence, which could be the closing sentence of your essay. Depending on the essay title, it could be a statement about a character: T.J. is a complex character as, despite his many weaknesses and wrongdoings, the reader ultimately feels great sympathy for his vulnerability and naivety; an opinion about setting: The land and its history give the Logan children a sense of self-worth and of family tradition which sets them apart from their neighbours; or a judgement on a theme: Mildred Taylor shows her reader how the racist views, prevalent in the southern state of Mississippi in the 1930s, affected the lives of one black family and their neighbours.
- Make a short essay plan. Use the first paragraph to introduce the argument you wish to make. In the following paragraphs develop this argument with details, examples and other possible points of view. Sum up your argument in the last paragraph. Check you have answered the question.
- Write the essay, remembering all the time the central point you are making.
- On completion, go back over what you have written to eliminate careless errors and improve expression. Read it aloud to yourself, or, if you are feeling more confident, to a relative or friend.

If you can, try to type your essay using a word processor. This will allow you to correct and improve your writing without spoiling its appearance.

Examination essay

The essay written in an examination often carries more marks than the coursework essay even though it is written under considerable time pressure.

In the revision period build up notes on various aspects of the text you are using. Fortunately, in acquiring this set of York Notes on *Roll of Thunder, Hear My Cry*, you have made a prudent beginning! York Notes are set out to give you vital information and help you to construct your personal overview of the text.

Make notes with appropriate quotations about the key issues of the set text. Go into the examination knowing your text and having a clear set of opinions about it.

In the examination

In most English Literature examinations you can take in copies of your set books. This in an enormous advantage although it may lull you into a false sense of security. Beware! There is simply not enough time in an examination to read the book from scratch.

- Read the question paper carefully and remind yourself what you have to do.
- Look at the questions on your set texts to select the one that most interests you and mentally work out the points you wish to stress.
- Remind yourself of the time available and how you are going to use it.
- Briefly map out a short plan in note form that will keep your writing on track and illustrate the key argument you want to make.
- Then set about writing it.
- When you have finished, check through to eliminate errors.

To summarise,
these are the
keys to success:

- Know the text
- Have a clear understanding of and opinions on the storyline, characters, setting, themes and writer's concerns
- Select the right material
- Plan and write a clear response, continually bearing the question in mind

SAMPLE ESSAY PLAN

A typical essay question on *Roll of Thunder, Hear My Cry* is followed by a sample essay plan in note form. This does not present the only answer to the question, merely one answer. Do not be afraid to include your own ideas, and leave out some of those in the sample! Remember that quotations are essential to prove and illustrate the points you make.

Write about the importance of family in *Roll of Thunder, Hear My Cry*.

Introduction

- Mildred Taylor wanted to show 'a family united in love and self-respect'. So she created the Logan family, who are presented as a role model for family life.

Part 1

The guiding role of parents
- Mama and Papa teach their children by example (Mama covers books, Papa won't shop at Wallace store)
- Firm discipline (Papa beats children for visiting Wallace store)
- Parents listen and give advice (Papa advises Cassie about Lillian Jean and Stacey about Jeremy, Mama tells Cassie about racism)
- Both parents actively promote education (Mama supervises homework, Papa buys books for Christmas presents)
- Parents are caring and supportive of each other (when Mama loses her job, when Papa is injured)

- Extended family: Big Ma adds to stability of environment and increases awareness of family history

Part 2
The response of the Logan children
- They respect and love their parents (as Cassie shows for her mother during the preparations for church)
- Children seek parental approval (Cassie explains to her mother about the books)
- Children accept parents' right to punish when appropriate (no resentment after beating from Papa)
- Children care for each other (Stacey organises revenge on bus to redress Little Man's hurt, Cassie is angry with T.J. when he takes Stacey's coat)
- Cassie and Stacey bemused by Jeremy's detachment from his family

Part 3
Other families – black
- Usually seen in relation to the Logans
- Averys are poorer than Logans, and are unable to instil discipline in T.J. However, the strength of feeling within the family is clear (attempts to protect T.J. from lynch mob)
- Mr Turner is also a poor sharecropper. Despite raising his children as a single parent, he provides a supportive family environment. He prevents his children from going to the Wallace store and presumably encourages his son, Moe, in his education (walks several miles to school each day)
- Both black families try to make the best of difficult situations

Part 4
Other families – white
- Very little information; usually negative
- The Simms, excepting Jeremy, learn their racist behaviour from their father (Cassie and Lillian Jean on the sidewalk). This bigotry seems to lead directly to violence and crime (Cassie's attack on Lillian Jean,

R.W. and Melvin's befriending of T.J. followed by
the violent Barnett robbery and T.J.'s beating and
possible execution)
- The Wallaces are, as a family, also racist and also
  violent (attack on Papa, Stacey and Mr Morrison)
- Mr Granger's family are not seen, but the influence
  of his mother is made clear (Old South values)
- Mr Jamison and his wife are a rare positive image of
  a white family, discussing and agreeing on all
  important issues that affect them

Conclusion   The family is central to the story. The Logans are
presented as a model family against which the others
are contrasted.

Mildred Taylor seems to be saying that children will be
well adjusted if their parents are. If parents are full of
hatred, their children will, in turn, hate.

Further questions

Here are four more common questions on the novel.
Work out what your answer would be, always being
sure to draw up a plan first.

1 What have you learnt about life in the southern state
  of Mississippi from reading *Roll of Thunder, Hear
  My Cry*?
2 To what extent does Mildred Taylor portray T.J. as
  being a victim of the times?
3 In the final line of the book Cassie cries for the land.
  Write about the importance of the land throughout
  the story.
4 Choose three of the following characters. Explain
  the influence they have on Cassie and how she feels
  towards them: Big Ma, Stacey, Lillian Jean or Uncle
  Hammer.

PART FIVE

CULTURAL CONNECTIONS

BROADER PERSPECTIVES

An understanding of slavery is essential if you are to grasp the main issues raised by *Roll of Thunder, Hear My Cry*. Many slaves wrote or dictated accounts of their experiences of legal bondage in the southern states. These accounts are known as slave narratives. The only one known to be written by a woman is Harriet Jacob's *Incidents in the Life of a Slave Girl* which was published under the pseudonym of Linda Brent in 1861.

Roll of Thunder, Hear My Cry is frequently compared to *To Kill A Mockingbird* (1960), a novel written by a white woman called Harper Lee. It is set in Alabama, a state that borders Mississippi, and is told from the viewpoint of a young white girl, Scout. Like *Roll of Thunder, Hear My Cry*, the action of the story takes place in the 1930s and strongly reflects the racist attitudes of those times.

The Color Purple (1982) by Alice Walker is a sensitive and touching novel, written in the form of a series of letters, detailing the life of Celie and set in the Deep South between the wars. *The Color Purple* is also a highly successful film, produced by Steven Spielberg.

You can also follow the fortunes of the Logan family in Mildred Taylor's sequel *Let the Circle be Unbroken* (1981).

character Characters are the invented, imaginary persons in a dramatic or narrative work.

dialect Local versions of a language spoken in different areas.

first person narrative The narrator speaks of himself as 'I' and is generally a character in the story. This differs from third-person narrative in which the narrator describes the characters as 'he', 'she' or 'they'.

structure The overall principle of organisation in a work of literature.

style The characteristic manner in which a writer expresses herself, or the particular manner of an individual literary work.

theme A central idea explored in a text, either explicitly or implicitly. A text may contain several themes or thematic interests.

TEST ANSWERS

TEST YOURSELF (Chapters 1–3)

A...
1 Papa *(Chapter 1)*
2 T.J. *(Chapter 1)*
3 Mama *(Chapter 1)*
4 Mr Lanier *(Chapter 2)*
5 Papa *(Chapter 2)*
6 Cassie *(Chapter 3)*
7 Jeremy *(Chapter 1)*
8 Mama *(Chapter 1)*
9 John Henry Berry *(Chapter 2)*

TEST YOURSELF (Chapters 4–6)

A...
1 Melvin Simms *(Chapter 4)*
2 Mr Morrison *(Chapter 4)*
3 Mr Turner *(Chapter 4)*
4 T.J. *(Chapter 5)*
5 Mr Barnett *(Chapter 5)*
6 Mama *(Chapter 6)*
7 Mr Berry *(Chapter 4)*
8 Uncle Hammer *(Chapter 6)*

TEST YOURSELF (Chapters 7–9)

A...
1 Uncle Hammer *(Chapter 7)*
2 Mr Morrison *(Chapter 7)*
3 Mr Jamison *(Chapter 7)*
4 Papa *(Chapter 8)*
5 Lillian Jean *(Chapter 8)*
6 T.J. *(Chapter 8)*
7 The Wallaces *(Chapter 7)*
8 Jeremy *(Chapter 7)*
9 Melvin and R.W. Simms *(Chapter 9)*

TEST YOURSELF (Chapter 10–12)

A...
1 Mr Morrison *(Chapter 10)*
2 Jeremy *(Chapter 10)*
3 Uncle Hammer *(Chapter 10)*
4 T.J. *(Chapter 11)*
5 Mr Jamison *(Chapter 12)*
6 Cassie *(Chapter 12)*
7 Uncle Hammer *(Chapter 10)*
8 Mr Granger *(Chapter 10)*